PORT SIDE PIRATES!

written by Oscar Seaworthy

illustrated by Debbie Harter

Barefoot Books
Celebrating Art and Story

When I was young I had some fun
The day I went to sea.
I jumped on board a pirate ship,
And the captain said to me:

Oh we go this way, that way,
Port side, starboard
over the deep blue sea!

I sailed with you to Timbuktu
The day I went to sea.
I lived on board a pirate ship,
And the captain said to me:

Oh we go this way, that way,
Port side, starboard
over the deep blue sea!

The west wind's force blew us off course
The day I went to sea.
I lived on board a pirate ship,
And the captain said to me:

Oh we go this way, that way,
Port side, starboard
over the deep blue sea!

There she blows!

We hit a storm, our sails were torn
The day I went to sea.
I lived on board a pirate ship,
And the captain said to me:

Oh we go this way, that way,
Port side, starboard
over the deep blue sea!

The first mate roared, "man overboard!"
The day I went to sea.
I lived on board a pirate ship,
And the captain said to me:

Oh we go this way, that way,
Port side, starboard
over the deep blue sea!

Land ahoy!

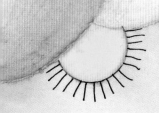

The storm blew out, we looked about
The day I went to sea.
I lived on board a pirate ship,
And the captain said to me:

Oh we go this way, that way,
Port side, starboard
over the deep blue sea!

From the front deck, we saw a wreck
The day I went to sea.
I lived on board a pirate ship,
And the captain said to me:

Oh we go this way, that way,
Port side, starboard
over the deep blue sea!

We had no fear, we sailed up near
The day I went to sea.
I lived on board a pirate ship,
And the captain said to me:

Oh we go this way, that way,
Port side, starboard
over the deep blue sea!

We found a hoard of gold on board
The day I went to sea.
I lived on board a pirate ship,
And the captain said to me:

Oh we go this way, that way,
Port side, starboard
over the deep blue sea!

Pieces of eight!

We weighed and measured
all our treasure
The day I went to sea.
I lived on board a pirate ship,
And the captain said to me:

Oh we go this way, that way,
Port side, starboard
over the deep blue sea!

We sang this song the whole day long
The day I went to sea.
Oh, the pirate's life is full of fun,
The pirate's life for me!

Oh we go this way, that way,
Port side, starboard
the pirate's life for me!

Aye, aye!

the Pirate's Galleon

1   sail
2   crow's nest
3   mast
4   forecastle
5   figurehead
6   bow
7   anchor
8   port side
9   starboard
10 hold
11 rat
12 ratlines
13 ship's cat
14 rigging
15 Jolly Roger
16 stern lantern
17 aftcastle
18 captain's cabin
19 cabin boy
20 deck
21 stern
22 rudder
23 hatch
24 hull
25 helm

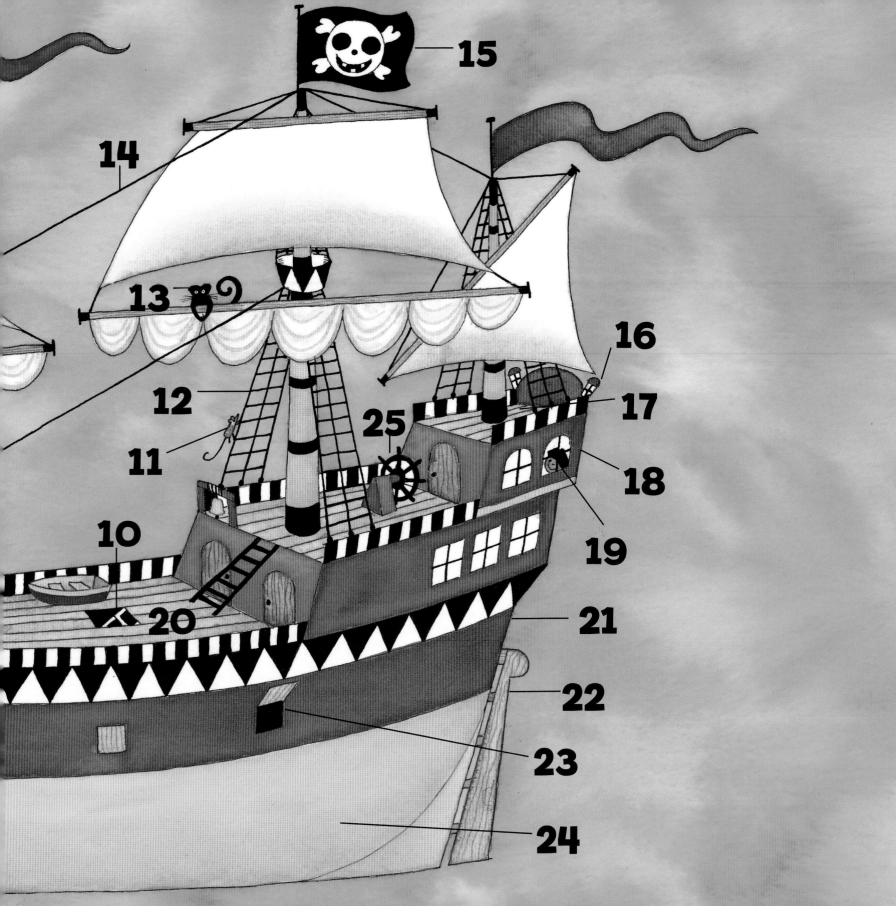

Pirate Ships

Pirates needed ships that were fast, seaworthy and easy to steer. Here are some of the ships that were used by pirates:

Galleons had two or more decks, three masts with square sails, and could hold over seventy cannons! The ship in this book is a galleon.

Sloops were small ships with large sails. Pirates used this ship because it could make quick turns.

Brigantines were very fast ships that were used as both merchant ships and naval ships.

Junks were ships that had curved sails held by bamboo, which is very strong.

Longboats were ships pulled by oarsmen. These ships were very important to the Vikings.

Pirates around the world

Dutch pirates were known as vrijbuiters. This word comes from combining *vrij* meaning *free* and *buiter* meaning *looter*. In English, a vrijbuiter is a freebooter. In French, he is a flibustier.

The pirates of the **Caribbean** are probably the most famous pirates. They came from England, Spain, and France. Piracy started in this area because of fights over different trade routes.

Pirates in the **West Indies** were called buccaneers. They started out as French sailors who raided Spanish ships during times of war. Then they went out on their own, claiming the seas for themselves.

Pirates from **East Asia** were known as wokou, which came from the combination of *wo* meaning *Japanese*, and *kou* meaning *bandit*. Their reign of piracy began in the 13th century. There are still many pirates today in southeast Asia.

Vikings were seafaring explorers and warriors from **Scandinavia**. Vikings were bold raiders and pillagers but they also worked hard, earning their living through trading. The word viking means *person of the bay*.

Famous Pirates

There have been pirates for as long as there have been ships. Here are some of the most famous ones:

Edward Teach was nicknamed Blackbeard because his bushy beard covered almost all of his face. He was one of the most infamous pirates to ever sail the seven seas. Born in England, he captained the ship Queen Anne's Revenge, which he captured from the French navy in the Caribbean.

Grace O'Malley left her home in Ireland and began accompanying her father on his voyages as a sailor at a young age, and soon she was known as a powerful pirate. At one time she was condemned to death, but Queen Elizabeth I pardoned her after they met.

William Kidd was born in Scotland and was originally the captain of The Blessed William. He sailed the Caribbean, fighting illegal pirates, until he himself became one. There is a legend that Captain Kidd left buried treasure — people have searched for it since his death.

Anne Bonny is the most famous female pirate. Originally from Ireland, she dressed as a man while she was at sea, gaining the respect of her fellow sailors. Even when she was discovered to be a woman, she continued to be admired for her skill and courage, ruling the waters of the Caribbean.

The **Barbarossa Brothers**, Khayr ad-Din and his brother Aruj, were Turkish pirates who ruled the Barbary Coast of North Africa. Aruj died in battle in 1518, but Khayr ad-Din remained a pirate. He was brave and determined, and went on to attack whole fleets, rather than single ships.

Port Side Pirates

Trad. arr. Mark Collins

For Jen, Colby and Tyler — yo, ho, ho! — O. S.

For Finlay — D. H.

Barefoot Books
124 Walcot Street
Bath, BA1 5BG, UK

Barefoot Books
2067 Massachusetts Ave
Cambridge, MA 02140, USA

With thanks to Mark Collins for lead and backing vocals, arrangements and synthesiser; Robin Davies for
bass guitar; Alex Hutchings for lead and rhythm guitar; and Charlotte Bell, Jessica Bell, Emily Cook,
Christina Daisley, Hannah Daisley, Henrietta Feeny, Ben Richer and Euan Shanahan for the children's choir

This book has been printed on 100% acid-free paper

This book was typeset in Aunt Mildred, Slappy and Kingdom
The illustrations were prepared in paint,
pen and ink, and crayon

Paperback ISBN 978-1-84686-153-6

First published in Great Britain
by Barefoot Books, Ltd
and in the United States of America
by Barefoot Books, Inc in 2007
This paperback first published in 2008

Graphic design by Louise Millar, London
Reproduction by Grafiscan, Verona
Printed and bound in China by Printplus, Ltd

The Library of Congress cataloged the hardcover edition as follows:

Seaworthy, Oscar.
  Port side pirates / Oscar Seaworthy ; [illustrated by] Debbie Harter.
    p. cm.
  ISBN 978-1-84686-062-1 (alk. paper)
  1. Pirates--Poetry. I. Harter, Debbie, ill. II. Title.

PS3619.E258P67 2007
811'.6--dc22

2006038845

British Cataloguing-in-Publication Data:
a catalogue record for this book is available from the British Library

1 3 5 7 9 8 6 4 2